. . . *for parents and teachers*

Children need preparation for a hospital experience — explanations of what will happen and why, and how they will feel. In addition to emotional support, they need suggestions for behaviors that are acceptable as demonstrated by adults around them. Parents, teachers, and professionals can use a book like *The Hospital Scares Me* to facilitate children's feeling of mastery over a hospital experience.

The approach of this book is pleasant yet realistic. It is useful not only prior to admission, but also during or after a hospital visit — to help an "unprepared" child cope more effectively with current or past hospital events. This book also will demystify the hospital for siblings or classmates of a hospitalized child. It is never too late to educate children about the hospital experience.

JERRIANN MYERS WILSON
DIRECTOR, CHILD LIFE
DEPARTMENT
THE JOHNS HOPKINS HOSPITAL
CHILDREN'S CENTER

The authors would like to acknowledge the assistance of The
Institute for Child Health at London University, Gower's Library
at the National Hospital for Nervous Diseases, and the Rockefeller
Medical Library at Alexandra House in England.

Library of Congress Number: 79-23886

2 3 4 5 6 7 8 9 0 84 83 82 81

Library of Congress Cataloging in Publication Data

Hogan, Paula Z
  The hospital scares me.

  SUMMARY: After being rushed to the hospital
with a broken ankle, Dan gradually grows less afraid
as he receives emotional support and explanations
of everything that happens to him.
  [1. Hospitals — Fiction. 2. Medical care —
Fiction. 3. Fractures — Fiction] I. Hogan, Kirk,
joint author. II. Thelen, Mary. III. Title.
PZ7.H68313Ho   [E]   79-23886
ISBN 0-8172-1351-1 lib. bdg.

THE HOSPITAL SCARES ME

by Paula Z. Hogan and Kirk Hogan, M.D.

illustrated by Mary Thelen

introduction by Jerriann Myers Wilson

RAINTREE CHILDRENS BOOKS
Milwaukee • Toronto • Melbourne • London

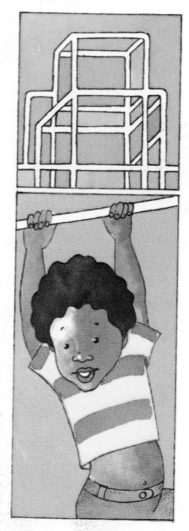

Bit by bit, Dan swung himself across the monkey bars.

"Hey, look at me!" called his sister Dianne from somewhere behind him.

Dan dangled in midair. As he twisted around, he lost his grip on the bar above him.

Thud! Dan hit the ground. A sharp pain stabbed his ankle.

"Oh, Dan!" Dianne ran to his side. "What happened?"

Tears were starting to roll down Dan's cheeks. "I . . . I can't get up," he groaned.

"You stay right here," she said. "I'm going to get help."

By the time she came running back with their mother, Dan's ankle was big and puffy.

Mrs. Martin looked at it carefully, then turned to Dianne. "You stay with Dan while I call a taxi. I'm taking Dan to the hospital."

"But I don't want to go there," Dan cried. "The hospital scares me."

"I'm not crazy about going there myself," said his mother, squeezing his hand. "But it's the only place where we can get that ankle taken care of. Don't worry, Dan — I'll be right there with you."

A short time later, the taxi was pulling up at the hospital door.

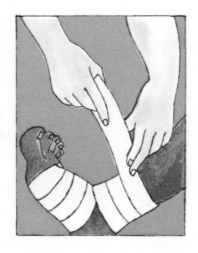

A man and a woman came out, helped Dan onto a cart, and wheeled him into a small room.

Dan looked around. He didn't like this place. It was full of bright lights, strange tools, and people in funny clothes.

Dan was ready to cry again, when a nurse walked over to him.

"I'll bet you don't feel too good right now," she said.

"You're r-right," he answered.

"I don't blame you! Why don't you tell me how you hurt your leg? While you talk, I'm going to put a temporary bandage on this leg."

As Dan talked and watched the nurse, he felt a little less like crying. Not long after she had finished bandaging his ankle, a man popped his head in the doorway.

"Hi, I'm Dr. Waters," the man said. "You must be Dan Martin, the famous king of the monkey bars."

"I used to be pretty good," Dan admitted, watching as Dr. Waters examined his ankle. "But now —"

"You'll be as good as ever once we make your ankle well," Dr. Waters said. "Now, the first thing we're going to do is take an X ray."

"Oh, no — that sounds scary."

"It won't hurt," the doctor promised. "It's just like having your picture taken."

A friendly man named Ben wheeled Dan to the X-ray room. They pretended the cart was a race car. Dan's mother walked along beside them. She waited in the hall while Ben took Dan inside the X-ray room.

11

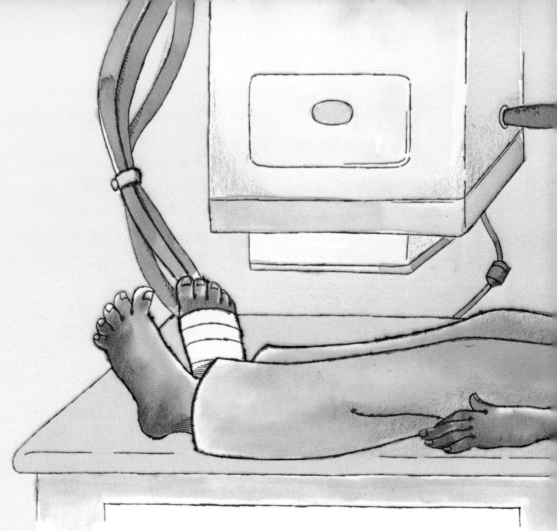

"Look at all these big machines," said
Dan.

"They're here to help you, not hurt
you," said Ben.

He helped Dan onto a table. A woman
asked him to hold still and took some
quick pictures of his ankle.

"It didn't hurt at all," Dan told his

mother when he and Ben came back out
into the hall.

A little later, Dr. Waters brought in
Dan's X rays and showed them to Dan and
his mother.

"I'm going to call in a bone doctor,"
he told them. "In the meantime, the
nurse will give Dan an injection to help
the pain."

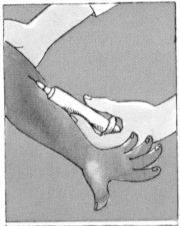

"You mean a shot?" Dan cried. "I hate shots!"

"I know just how you feel," said his mother. "Here, squeeze my hand, and we'll count together. It'll be over before you know it. Go ahead and cry if it will make you feel better."

The nurse gave Dan the injection. It stung a little, but not enough to make him cry.

Dan's ankle was feeling a lot better by the time another man walked into the room.

"I'm Dr. Chun," he said. "I've been looking at your X rays. I want to show you what I'm going to do, Dan." He pointed to an X ray. "See where that break is?"

Dan nodded.

"That break won't heal well unless I work on it right away. I'll get you a room on the children's floor of this hospital. I know this is all very strange to you, Dan, but there's nothing to be afraid of."

"Okay," said Dan. "But I'm still afraid!"

Dan and his mother went upstairs to his room.

A nurse helped him undress and gave him a gown to wear.

"Couldn't I keep my own clothes on?" Dan asked.

"This is just for the operation," the nurse said. "Maybe later you can put your own clothes back on."

As the nurse was helping Dan into bed, Dan's father arrived.

"I came over as soon as I could," he said. "How do you feel, Dan?"

"Scared!"

"You look really brave to me!"

Right behind Dan's father was a woman. "Hello," she said. "My name is Dr. Hood. I will help you fall into a special sleep."

"I'm not tired," said Dan. "Why do I have to go to sleep?"

"So it won't hurt while Dr. Chun is fixing your ankle," she answered. "I'll be watching over you the whole time. You'll wake up when everything's over."

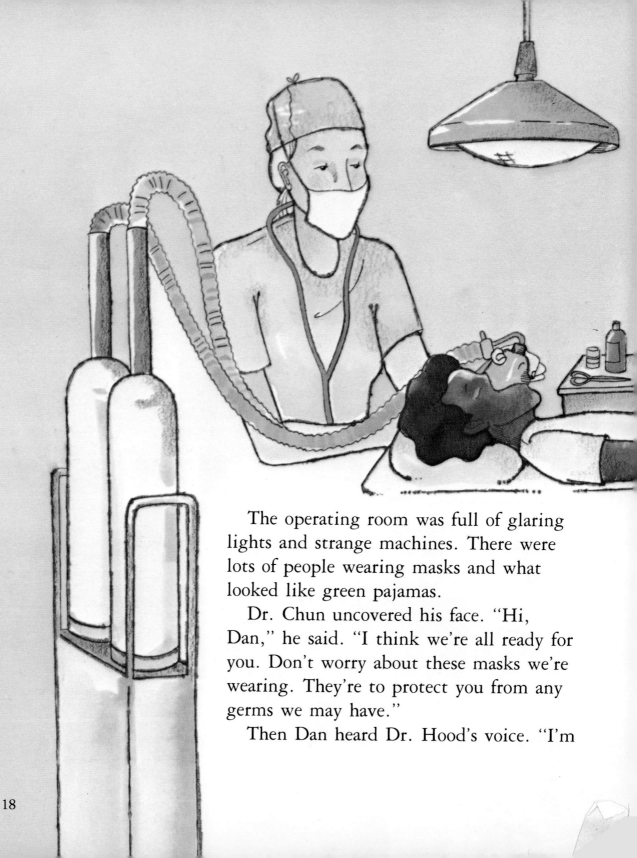

The operating room was full of glaring
lights and strange machines. There were
lots of people wearing masks and what
looked like green pajamas.

Dr. Chun uncovered his face. "Hi,
Dan," he said. "I think we're all ready for
you. Don't worry about these masks we're
wearing. They're to protect you from any
germs we may have."

Then Dan heard Dr. Hood's voice. "I'm

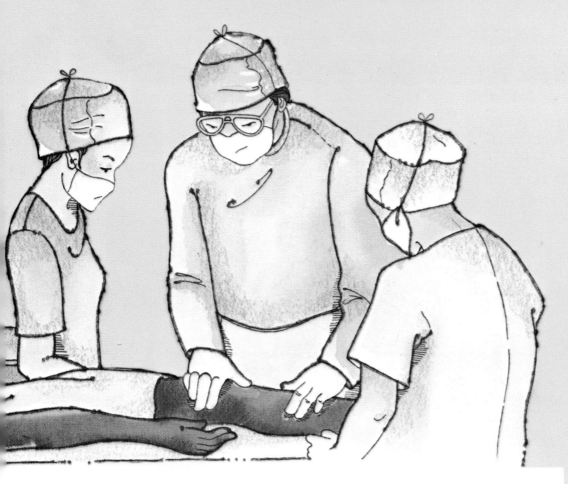

going to hold this black mask over your
mouth and nose, Dan. I want you to
breathe slowly."

Dan did what she told him. A funny
smell came from the mask.

"Pretend you're an astronaut," Dr. Hood
suggested. "The earth is getting farther
away. .... Just ahead is the moon . . ."

Maybe I'll land . . . on Mars, Dan
thought as he fell into a deep sleep.

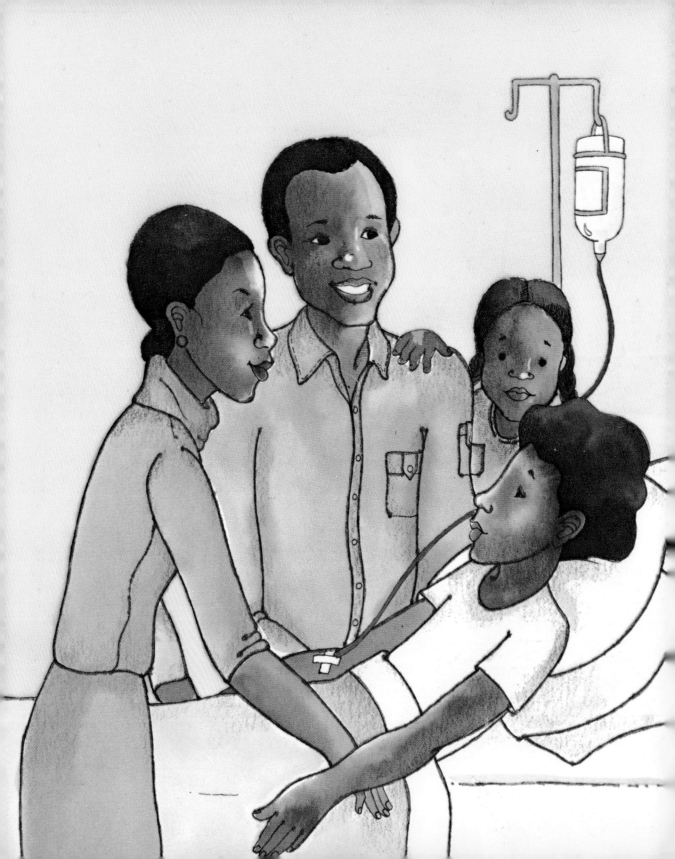

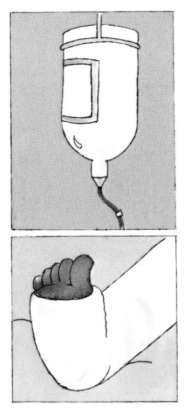

When Dan opened his eyes, he was back in his hospital room. His parents were sitting next to his bed. Dianne was there too, talking to the boy in the next bed.

Dan felt strange. His leg was in a big cast. It was up in the air, resting on pillows. On his hand was a bandage with a tube coming out. The tube led to a bottle hanging beside his bed.

"How are you doing?" asked his mother.

Dan yawned. "My leg feels sore in this cast. And what's this bottle for?"

"I asked the nurse," his father said. "She said it's a special medicine to keep you from getting an infection."

"And your leg is in that cast so it will heal the right way," said his mother. "Dr. Chun says that everything is going very well."

Dianne came over. "Do you want some juice? The nurse said you could have some."

"Later," said Dan. "I'm kind of tired. . . ."

"Hi," called the boy in the next bed. "My name's Mike. Do you want to watch TV?"

"Sure . . ." Dan answered, but in another minute he was fast asleep.

Dan woke up the next morning to find a new nurse standing over him.

"Are you ready for a little breakfast, Dan?" she asked. "Your mom and dad told me to tell you they'd be here right after breakfast."

"Okay," Dan said as the nurse moved his bed up. "But what happened to the other nurse?"

"She's home right now. She'll be back this afternoon." The nurse brought in two breakfast trays for Dan and Mike.

Dan turned to Mike. "How come you don't have a cast on *your* leg?" he asked.

"Because there's nothing wrong with my leg," Mike answered. "It's my stomach. I had bad pains there, and I just had an operation." Mike showed Dan the bandage on his stomach.

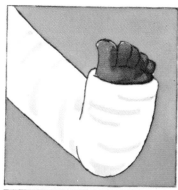

As Dan was finishing breakfast, Dr. Chun walked in.

"Good morning," he said. "How's your ankle feel?"

"I can't move it, and it's hot."

Dr. Chun nodded. "Can you wiggle your toes?"

Dan moved his toes.

"You're doing fine," said Dr. Chun. "You just take it easy and keep up the good work. Soon you'll be able to go home."

On his way out, Dr. Chun almost bumped into Dan's parents. Dan's father could only stay for a little while, but Dan's mother stayed with him all day.

"Where's Dianne?" asked Dan.

"In school," said Mrs. Martin.

"Oh, school," Dan groaned. "How long do I have to stay here? I'm going to get so far behind in school that the other kids will think I'm dumb when I get back."

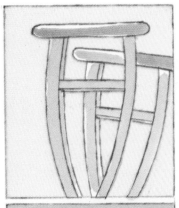

"I called your teacher," said his mother. "He's going to send me your homework. There's a special worker right here at the hospital who will help you with it. You can't escape homework just by breaking your ankle, you know!"

Dan smiled.

As the days passed he began to feel better and better. The nurse took the bandage from his hand. Dr. Chun put a walking cast on his leg and helped him practice walking with crutches. Dan could walk to the playroom and visit the other kids.

His parents visited him every day. Sometimes Dianne came too and brought him his favorite puzzles and toys. He did a little homework in the playroom every day. Friends and relatives sent him cards.

Still, Dan missed his house, his friends, and even school. Every day he asked Dr. Chun if he was ready to go home. Every day Dr. Chun showed him his X rays and explained how his ankle was healing.

At last the day came when Dan was well enough to go home. His mother helped him pack his things and brought a special sock to put over his cast. She and Dan said good-bye to the people who had taken care of him.

"I want to see you in two weeks," called Dr. Chun.

"Will you take my cast off then?" Dan asked.

"I just want to see how you're getting along. You'll have to keep the cast for a few months."

Dan was so happy to be home. Dianne had made a big Welcome Home sign for his room. His parents cooked hamburgers — Dan's favorite meal — for dinner.

The next morning, Dan took his time getting ready for school. "Do I really *have* to go to school with this thing on my leg?" he asked his mother.

"The doctor says you're well enough for school. You're not sick, you know. Hurry up, now, and have a good day."

When Dan got to his classroom, the teacher, Mr. Krull, asked him to tell the class about the hospital.

When he finished talking, a girl raised her hand. "May we write our names on Dan's cast?"

"That's up to him," said Mr. Krull.

"Sure," Dan laughed.

Everyone signed his cast, even Mr. Krull.

"Dan, weren't you scared to go to the hospital?" a boy asked.

Dan just smiled. "Sort of, even though going to the hospital wasn't so bad. But it's even better to be back!"